3.5°

JEFFERSON COLLEGE

3 6021 00039 0785

66-4310

D1276501

OK                                    66-4310

PZ4
.W632        Wibberley
Is           The Island of the
             angels.

JUNIOR COLLEGE DISTRICT OF
JEFFERSON COUNTY, MISSOURI
LIBRARY

# THE
# ISLAND
# OF
# THE
# ANGELS

*Other fiction by the same author*

A FEAST OF FREEDOM

THE MOUSE ON THE MOON

MRS. SEARWOOD'S SECRET WEAPON

THE MOUSE THAT ROARED

McGILLICUDDY McGOTHAM

TAKE ME TO YOUR PRESIDENT

BEWARE OF THE MOUSE

QUEST OF EXCALIBUR

STRANGER AT KILLKNOCK

# THE
# ISLAND
# OF
# THE
# ANGELS

*by*

*LEONARD*
*WIBBERLEY*

William Morrow & Co.　　New York 1965

Copyright © 1965 by Leonard Wibberley. All rights
reserved. Published simultaneously in the Dominion of
Canada by George J. McLeod Limited, Toronto. Printed
in the United States of America.

Second Printing, May 1965

Library of Congress Catalog Card Number 65-13578

# THE
# ISLAND
# OF
# THE
# ANGELS

## Chapter 1

It was a little before four o'clock in the morning—an hour until there would be any lightening of the horizon in the east to mark the coming of another day. The sky was dark and the sea below it darker still, so that the fisherman had the feeling that he was trapped in a globe of darkness from which he would escape only by a miracle. The miracle—the opening of the door which would let him out of this dark prison—would take place in the east when the dawn came.

All night long the fisherman had been working in his boat and had had only two glimpses of the stars through the pall of clouds overhead. A little before midnight he had seen three stars in a line which he knew were part of the constellation of Orion. And about an hour ago he had seen to the north of him four stars making a rough oblong which belonged to the constellation of the Plow. The sight of these had cheered him, for the stars were the lighthouses by which he guided himself in the dark, and a glimpse of them made him feel less lonely. He did not know the names of the constellations for he had never studied navigation and indeed had no education at all. But he gave the constellations names of his own. Orion he called The Man. The Plow he called The Saucepan.

His name was Francisco and he was a Mexican. He was an old man, well past fifty years of age, and for the last thirty years he had lived on the Island of the Angels off the coast of Baja California. Originally, when he first came to the island, there had been several other fishermen there. They had fished as he fished now, with a small, rough boat equipped with oars and a sail set on a mast which could be taken down. It was the sail known among the Americans as a dipping lugsail.

There was a boom or gaff which went from the bottom of the mast to the top corner of the sail, and when he wanted to tack his boat he had to lower the sail completely and raise it again when he had rowed the boat across the wind to the new direction. This was old-fashioned equipment and the other fishermen on the Island of the Angels had fitted their boats after a while with outboard engines. They had then become dependent on the mainland for gasoline and so they had left the island. But Francisco did not like the mainland and he did not like to be dependent on others.

"A man does not have to buy the wind," he said, reflecting on what had happened to the others. "When you have to buy something to move your boat you have not made an improvement. You have only made an entanglement."

He had been living alone on the island now for a quarter of a century and he had come to regard it as his island. He did not want anybody else on it. In a large, bustling, hurrying, noisy world, he, Francisco Malaga, had found a place alone. The thought pleased him. How many millions of people there were in the world much wealthier than he who had not any place of their own unless they were rich enough to buy it—and then it was only a house, or perhaps a house with a few acres around it. It was not an island. In the whole world, he decided, there were perhaps not more than a hundred men who owned islands.

"It is better to own an island than anything in the world," he said. "An island with no one on it but oneself. I will tell you something," he continued, addressing his boat or perhaps the general darkness around him, "a man is born alone and he dies alone and anything in between that appears to decrease this loneliness is purely a deception. It is the natural state of man to be solitary."

It had become a habit of Francisco's to talk aloud in this manner to the stars, the boat, the darkness, his oars, his mast, his sail, or even the fish he caught. Other men had the same thoughts running through their minds but were forced by society to remain silent. There was no such compunction laid on Francisco. He could speak when he wished and remain silent when he wished, and the arrangement suited him.

He had been fishing that night with a long line. The line was about half a mile in length and had hooks set six feet apart. That made over four hundred hooks which he always baited, when he fished in this manner, in the cool of the evening. Then he laid out the line at night, two or three miles off the island, and then pulled it in at dawn to discover his catch. He salted the fish he caught, packed them in barrels, and took them to the mainland to sell when he had a sufficient cargo. Sometimes there was not a single fish worth catching on the whole half-mile of line. There might be a skate or a shark or a bonita or other fish of this kind which were good only for bait. It was the groupers that sold well, and often he could fish for a week with a hand line and not take a single grouper.

A flash of light appeared in the sky to his left and he turned quickly to see a falling star trail across the blackness and then be gone in a moment. He was beginning to pull in his line when he saw this. He wrapped the line around the tholepins of his boat, bowed his head, and held his hands together.

"Eternal rest give unto him, Oh Lord, and let the perpetual light shine upon him." He said this because it was the prayer for the newly dead and everybody in Mexico knew that a falling star marked the death of a man who had been a heavy sinner, and whose soul was plunging into Hell. Therefore it was necessary to say the prayer in the hope that something might be found at the man's judgment which would save him from eternal damnation.

When he had finished the prayer he felt cold quite suddenly and not at ease and he looked around him to see what was disturbing him. There was nothing about but the darkness, and the only sound was the slapping of the water against the sides of the boat. He remained very quiet for a moment feeling its movement. He made every nerve in his body attend to the motion because what had made him uneasy might have been waves coming from a new direction and forerunning a storm. The boat seemed easy in the water and he looked around again but saw nothing.

"Nonetheless, something has happened," he said. "There is a change and I have had a warning. But I do not know what the change is."

He continued thinking very deeply about his problem while hauling in his line. There were two grouper on the line, one of fifty kilos and one of about thirty. It was a good catch for the night. When he had got the line back into the two tubs in which it was coiled, he stood up in the boat and saw a faint glistening on the dark water to the east. When he sat down the glistening was gone and he knew it was the dawn.

"Thank God for the day," he said. "With the light a man is not so cold." This was quite true. The darkest hour was three in the morning and it was always the coldest. He could tell the time by the degree of cold. But as soon as there was a smear of light on the water he would begin immediately to feel warmer.

He waited now for the wind. The sun rose over the mainland, which was all desert except for the little town of Colonia Madre. As soon as the sun hit the desert it warmed the air and this warm air, rising, drew in the cold air from the ocean and created a favorable wind to take him back to the Island of the Angels. As the light increased over the land he saw a dim cobweb shape of the desert mountain—and nearer, but still vague, his own island.

He bailed the boat with a small, battered, enamel saucepan, rowed it around so that its head lay pointed half a mile north of his island and then raised his mast and sail. The sail was cut from another which he had bought second-hand and it was old and had two large patches on it. Still it served well in a moderate wind, and with a boat of his size he would carry no sail at all in a heavy wind. When the sail was up it flopped about solemnly until he had taken the sheet at the lower corner and pulled it in a little.

Then the sail filled and the boat stopped rocking and moved with a gliding motion through the water.

Francisco shifted his tubs with the heavy wet line in them up to windward and pulled the two big groupers in that direction also to trim the boat. Then he settled down with the tiller in his hand. The wind would take him home in an hour and when he got there he would know, he decided, something more of the change which he felt was about to take place, and of which some warning had been sent by the falling star.

## Chapter 2

The dawn—the door by which the fisherman was to escape from the dark bowl of the night—was fully opened as he approached the Island of the Angels. He had set a course to the north of the island knowing that the current combining with the tide which was now flowing would carry him down onto it. From a cobweb on the horizon it had grown into a solid which had at this hour the appearance of a rough piece of crystal. The light struck on the ridges as on the facets of a diamond, and the shadows were of a darkness between gray and black.

Francisco always loved this particular view of the island and believed that it was because of this appearance that it had been given the name of the Island of the Angels for there was a sparkling as from heaven on the contours of the hills. In actuality the island was truly a desert island; not the desert island of South Sea romances but a harsh, rocky protrusion with a thin soil on it which supported wild grass and cactus. In the spring, which was the only season when rain fell in that area, the grass was green and if there was an exceptionally heavy rain, wild lupines grew among the rocks. But this show of green and blue lasted for only a few weeks—and then all the vegetation, except the cacti, died off and the island became as tawny as the hide of a lion.

On the north end there was a cliff of rocks with two reefs running out from it. Behind the southernmost of these two reefs was a small bay, the beach being of stones but with a little sand above the highwater mark. It was here that Francisco had his house. It lay at the back of the bay, one wall being composed of natural rock, the others of rough planks and pieces of galvanized iron hammered together in an

outrageous caricature of a dwelling. Some of the
pieces of the house were indeed flattened-out kero-
sene cans, but they served the purpose of keeping out
the wind; and as far as the fisherman was concerned
the house was as snug as a man might desire. It had
for Francisco the especial attraction that he had built
it himself and he owned it.

The ridge of the reef obscured the house as he
approached the bay. He stood up in his boat as he
always did, for the passage was difficult. He had
wind and sea behind him and a bar of rock to come
over. He stood because he could better feel the way
his boat was handling at this difficult point.

A big sea gathered behind him as he approached
the bar and he let the sheet of the mainsail go so that
the wind was spilled from it, the boat slowed, and the
wave passed underneath it. Immediately, he seized
the sheet, pulled it tight so that the sail was drawing,
and shot in over the bar behind the wave. He left the
tiller, ran forward, dropped an anchor, and the boat
snubbed on the line and turned quite prettily around
inside the bay to face wind and sea, safely home.

Francisco took down the mast and sail and paid
out on the anchor line until the boat was floating in
shallow water near the stony beach. He glanced

briefly at the beach, noted that some of the stones above the edge of the surf were wet and knew from this that the tide would soon ebb. He stepped into the water and carried ashore another anchor consisting of a large flat stone secured to a grass rope. He placed this on the beach and his boat was secure fore and aft—it would come to no trouble. Only then did he look around the cove and see something lying before the door of his shack.

The shack was a hundred yards away and he could not make out, at that distance, precisely what it was that lay before the door. But it seemed to be a bundle of rags.

"It cannot have been brought in by the sea," he said, "for the sea never reaches that far. Somebody has brought it. They may still be here." He looked around immediately at the scarred hills at the back of the bay and southward to where they disappeared behind a promontory of rock.

"This is the change I knew was coming," he said. As usual he spoke aloud. He decided to investigate the bundle and had walked halfway toward it before he realized that it was not merely a wad of old rags but a boy. He walked slowly to within a few feet of the boy and then stooped and stared down at him.

He was a very small boy even for a Mexican. He had on a poncho of rough wool. It was too big for him and so had given the impression of being a bundle of rags. His hands were hidden in the poncho and he was lying on his back with his eyes shut and his mouth half-open.

Francisco knelt down and touched the boy's cheek. The skin was very cold. He put his hand on the boy's chest and fancied, though he could not be sure, that there was some movement.

He was suddenly very frightened. It was plain that if the boy was not already dead he was dying and something must be done immediately to save him. He did not know what to do. He picked the boy up. The poncho was soaking wet and he carried the boy into the shack and laid him on a trestle bed made of a wooden frame on legs with rawhide stretched across the frame. He took the poncho off and also a pair of ragged khaki shorts which were the boy's only other garment. He put a blanket over him and tried to think what to do next.

Since the boy had not moved, he decided to rub him vigorously with the blanket to restore circulation. After a little while the boy opened his eyes. Francisco continued to rub him for a while but said nothing.

He had an iron pot in the corner on a wooden box and in this he lit a charcoal fire, heated some condensed milk mixed with water in a pan and brought some to the boy and made him drink it. When he had taken the first mouthful the boy started shuddering from either cold or fright, but Francisco made him drink the rest of the milk and he became quieter.

"Boy," said Francisco, "what is your name?"

"Juan," said the boy.

"Juan what?"

"Only Juan," replied the boy.

"How did you get here?"

"In a boat."

"Why did you come here?"

"A man was chasing me."

"Why was he chasing you?"

"I don't know."

"Did he chase you in another boat to this island?"

"Yes. He follows me everywhere." The boy sounded terrified.

"What does he look like?" asked the fisherman.

"He is dark and short," said the boy.

Suspicion began to form in Francisco's mind. "You stole something from him?" he asked.

"No," said the boy.

"He is your father?"

"No. I have no father. I think he wants to kill me," said the boy.

"You think these things because you have not been getting enough to eat," said the fisherman. "You are half-starved. Anyone can see that. And when people have been without enough food for a long time they are full of fear. Courage starts in the stomach. Where is this boat you say you came over here in?"

"It is somewhere on the rocks. It went on the rocks and I had to swim."

Francisco eyed the poncho of rough wool he had taken off the boy. He doubted that the boy could really swim but the poncho would float him until it became waterlogged. And since it was still full of the natural oil of the sheep, that would not take place for a long time.

"Go to sleep," he said. "I have some things to do." He walked to the door and was about to go through it when he turned to look at the boy and saw that his eyes were wide-open and full of terror. "Do not be afraid," he said. "This is my island. No one can touch you here." Then he shut the door and went out to look for the short, dark stranger.

The island was only three-quarters of a mile long and about half a mile wide. The only beach on it was the one on which Francisco had built his hut. The rest of the coastline was rocky and the center of the island was a series of tawny peaks and sharp ravines, so exposed to the weather and so lacking in moisture that only the quick, fierce growth of the desert could exist on it.

Francisco knew every acre of the island and walked purposely to the top of a peak from which he could survey the whole place. He had never worn shoes but his feet were tough, purposeful pads quite impervious to stones and thorns. The skin on them was like that on the neck of a turtle, leathery and wrinkled, and his toenails were, either from age or wear, reduced to little flints. His whole body had the toughness of his feet, which found a perfect match in his worn but hardy hands.

He walked up the hill, slightly crouched, moving fast but seemingly with little effort. While he walked he thought about the frightened boy and the falling star. The boy's fright was real enough for the boy to have taken a boat and come ten miles by night across the channel to the island. It had been a very dark night and there was no light on the island to guide the boy. He could easily have missed the island and been lost out to sea.

But what about the man the boy said had also

landed on the island? Had he also come in a boat
following the boy to the island? Or had he come
in the same boat as the boy and had the boy, trying
to escape from him, flung himself overboard in the
dark and struggled to the Island of the Angels?

Some part of the problem would be answered, Francisco decided, when he reached the peak of the hill he
was climbing. From the top he could see the whole
coastline of his island and would soon spot any boat
or boats that had landed on it.

When he reached the peak he squatted on his thin
haunches, squinted his eyes in the bright morning
sun, and went over the island as it were inch by inch.
He knew every feature of it. There was no movement
anywhere, though it would be possible for the other
man to hide in the shadows of the ravines. There was
no boat nor wreckage of a boat along the coastline.
The current flowed to the south and he looked in that
direction lest the boat the boy had come in had
drifted southward. But he saw nothing.

Then he turned to the east and looking into the sun
which now made a swathe of molten light on the
water he saw something that might have been a boat
with a man in it, but he could not be sure. There was
a short dark line on the water which appeared and

disappeared as it rose to the crest or dipped in the trough of the waves. It could be a boat or it could be the trunk of a tree. He watched it for a long time and then went down the hill to the hut and the boy.

On the way down he decided he would say nothing of this to the boy. Most questions answered themselves in time, he knew. He had only to wait and he would find out the true story of the boy and the man and the boy's fears.

## Chapter 3

When Francisco returned from the hill he was an-
noyed with himself for having delayed so long, for
already a few flies were beginning to collect around
the two grouper he had caught. He always gutted
and cleaned his catch as soon as he got it ashore,
however tired he might be, before the mounting sun,
with its swift head, had a chance of rendering the fish
stale. By this time the grouper should already be
salted down in the boxes and in his irritation at the

delay he ran across the beach without looking in at the boy. He grabbed the old fish knife from the bow of his boat, gave it a few angry scrapes on a flat stone and started cleaning the grouper.

He tackled the big one first. The dark scales on the side uppermost were already dull and dry. Some of the moisture had gone from the flesh underneath the skin and the taste would be strong. He could at least have remembered to put some wet kelp over the fish before leaving the boat and he had not even done this.

"Bah," he said, inserting the knife swiftly under the gillplates and sliding it up until he could feel the edge lodge between two sections of the backbone. "Why couldn't they leave me alone? Why did that boy have to come to my island? He will bring me nothing but trouble. I will have to nurse him now and I cannot fish and take care of him. He is not my problem. He is someone else's problem but I have to deal with him." He continued working away, getting angrier at this interruption of his solitary life which he felt he had not merited.

Dwelling on the wrong which the boy had done him by coming to his island, he was scowling when an hour later he had finished his work and carried the big fillets cut from the grouper back to his hut to put in the salt boxes. The greater part of the offal he threw in the sea, though he saved some, including the heads of the two fish, for bait. He was in such a bad mood that he jerked open the door and walked in without looking at the boy, who sat up in bed and stared at him in terror and then lay down again. For a moment, seeing the boy's terror, Francisco felt sorry for him. But then his anger returned and he worked with his back to him, salting the fish, and then made himself a cup of coffee, all the time keeping his back to the boy.

It was only when he had supped up half his cup of coffee that he turned around to the boy, prepared to snap at him if he said anything. But the boy was silent, lying on the bed, breathing very heavily and looking up at the ceiling.

"What's the matter? You feeling worse?" Francisco asked. His voice was surly. The boy did not answer. The fisherman put his coffee cup down and went over to the bed and put his hand on the boy's face. It was as hot as a stone left lying in the midday sun. The boy was breathing noisily, straining to draw in each breath. The fisherman caught a whiff of foul air coming from his mouth.

"Let me look at your throat," he said and there was fear in his voice. He turned the boy's head to the side so as to catch the light from the door. The boy opened his mouth and the fisherman put his finger in to depress the tongue and catch a glimpse of the throat.

The back of the throat was covered with a dirty yellow substance and the fisherman knew what was the matter. It was diphtheria, though he did not know this name for the disease—it was called rotten throat among the people of the countryside. And he knew two things about it. It was almost always fatal, and it was very catching. Only a doctor could treat it, and even in Colonia Madre on the mainland there was no doctor. There was a schoolteacher there who did all the doctoring required by the people. But Colonia Madre was ten miles away across the sea, three hours in his boat. That was a long journey for anyone in the boy's condition; nonetheless it would have to be made, for he could not treat the boy himself.

When he realized that he would have to make the journey with the boy, Francisco suddenly became very tired. He had been working for fourteen hours, most of the time in his boat on the ocean, and all he had eaten in that time was some cold beans wrapped in tortillas. He sat down on one of the fish boxes, put his head between his hands and screwed his eyes up tight as if by this to drive the tiredness out of his brain and his muscles. Then he got up slowly, and as he drank the rest of his coffee from the enamel mug, his eye fell on a bottle of tequilla standing in a corner of the hut.

He had bought it two months before and now there was scarcely a teaspoonful of it left. He decided to drink it to relieve his tiredness and give him some strength and was raising the bottle to his lips when it occurred to him that the boy needed strength more than he did. What was he to do? Drink the tequilla himself or give it to the boy? He poured the clear fluid into the bottom of his mug, added a little water from a barrel and gave it to the boy. The boy coughed when the fiery liquid touched his throat, coughed so convulsively that it seemed he must choke. Some of the membrane in the back of his throat came up and fell on the fisherman's hand and he wiped it off quickly on his trousers.

"Boy," he said, "you are very sick. I have to take you to the schoolteacher at Colonia Madre. Can you walk?"

The boy only looked at him terrified.

"Come," Francisco said. "You have to have courage. The schoolteacher will make you well."

"Let me stay here," said the boy.

"The schoolteacher will make you well."

"If I go back there, I will die," the boy replied. "Let me stay here."

"If you stay here, you will die," said the fisherman. "I will have to carry you."

He stepped outside the hut, leaving the door open, and a puff of warm air touched his cheek. He looked immediately up to the top of the hill behind the hut. There was a clump of sagebrush growing on the ridge and its stiff twigs were shaking. A little smear of yellow dust came off the top of the hill and blew down toward him. He looked up at the sky and saw little, thin shreds of clouds, very high up, moving swiftly out to sea. Then he went back into the hut.

"Let me stay here," whispered the boy as soon as Francisco was through the door again.

"God has willed that you stay here," said the fisherman. "The chubasco is blowing. We will not be able to leave the island for a week."

To his surprise, the boy smiled and closed his eyes and seemed to fall asleep.

## Chapter 4

The chubasco was a fiercely hot, drying wind which blew from the interior deserts of the mainland out to sea. Once it started, it usually lasted a week, blowing fitfully, sometimes attaining a velocity of forty or fifty miles an hour and then lulling to a moderate breeze. But the periods of comparative calm were short, scarcely an hour or so, and when the wind returned it came unexpectedly and with full strength. It howled over the Island of the Angels, hissing down the ravines as if they had suddenly been filled with foaming water and making a high shriek over the ridges. With it there was always dust or, rather, sand, stripped from the desert and forming, first of all, an obscurity or haze in the sky and then thickening until it darkened the sun and the whole island lay under a turbulent gloom.

When the chubasco started to blow, Francisco always remained in his hut for there was nothing else to be done. He was self-sufficient there, having beans, flour, oil, fish and water with which to feed himself. His hut, built up against the rock, was in the lee of the island from the desert gale and would escape the worst ravages of the wind and the dust. His boat was safe enough in the little bay though he would go out in the lull to check it. He passed the time sleeping or working on his gear—his fishing lines, his lobster traps, and the sail of his boat, which he always kept in the hut with him. The chubasco then did not normally worry him. It came and it went according to the will of God. When it was gone he resumed his fishing.

But he was worried about it now because of the boy who was so sick, and in the back of his mind was a fear that he might become sick himself. The boy's condition was highly contagious—and he had to live in the hut with him and take care of him.

"If we both become sick we will both die," he said aloud. Then he added, "Fear is what kills. If I am not afraid we can both live." He felt better when he had given himself this assurance. It was something to hold on to. Brave men did not die before their time and surely his time would not come when the life of the boy depended on him. God was not so merciless as that.

He was not hungry—he had had too much excitement to have any appetite—but he made himself some fried beans and two tortillas and ate them. Then he took some sacks and part of an old sail, made a bed for himself on the floor and lay down on it. He was asleep in an instant.

Several times while the fisherman was asleep the boy woke up. Each time he awoke frightened for he kept dreaming that he was being followed by the short, dark man who would be just about to seize him from behind by the shoulder. Then he would awake whimpering, beside himself with fright, and he would look up at the iron roof of the hut and not recognize where he was for the moment. Then he would see the fisherman lying on the floor and he would feel better.

The fisherman was dark and short, too, but not like the man who was after him. The fisherman had a fierce look but it did not frighten the boy. He had not shaved for some days and had a rough bristle of white about his face. It was not a beard but just the result of not having shaved and his dark skin showed through the short white hairs. He was curled up on the floor facing the boy and the boy was glad about that.

Each time he awoke, the boy saw the fisherman lying on the floor facing him. From this he decided that the fisherman would help him—and he began to love him. He was very weak and hot, and looking at the fisherman in one of his waking moments he began to cry, without making any noise. He wasn't crying because he was sick or weak or afraid. He had long since given up crying about such things. He cried from a deep yearning never to be separated from the fisherman and never to have to go away from this island. It seemed to him that he had been running all his life from one place to another and now he had found a place where he did not have to run any more.

He let the tears flow and looked at the fisherman

with adoration and tried to think of something he could do for him when he was well that would be so deep and important that the fisherman would not take him back to Colonia Madre. He sensed that the fisherman did not want him to stay on the island, for he liked to be alone. To be sure, the fisherman had not said anything to him about that but the boy knew this was the case, for he was a little animal who lived by his wits and he had developed to a high degree the ability to read the thoughts of others from their faces.

In Colonia Madre he had shined shoes for people for whatever they would give him. To shine shoes he had to know precisely the mood of the person who wore the shoes. People did not plan to have shoes shined. If they did, they shined them themselves. If they decided to let the boy shine their shoes, it was the decision of a moment, based entirely on their feelings at that time. It was important then for him to know those feelings and he was a master at divining them.

People who had won money in the weekly lottery would have their shoes shined, but only after they had had a little while to get over their excitement at winning the money. Until then they were impatient with everybody else's desires and only wanted the whole world to know that they had won the money. Then they calmed down and began to feel generous and would have their shoes shined. After that they became worried at spending the money and started quarreling with anybody they thought would take it away from them.

Again, people who were drinking would have their shoes shined if you did not ask them. You had to stay in the bar in a corner, not interfering, and wait patiently. After a while the man who was drinking would call, "Hey, boy. Come here and shine these shoes of mine." They would be generous and give him sometimes a whole peso. But when they went on drinking and saw the boy later, they cursed him and told him to get out of their way and not come whining around them.

People going to church never wanted their shoes shined. For one thing, they were always late for church and hadn't the time. Also they had brought only enough money to put in the collection plate and were often in a bad temper about having to part with that. Sometimes some North Americans passed through Colonia Madre, but it was never much use trying to shine their shoes. They didn't much care

what condition their shoes were in, and anyway they were always in a hurry and hadn't the time to wait for a shine.

They usually stopped to eat at Ah Fong's restaurant, though sometimes, having first looked through the window, they would go into the Estralita Café, where Mexican food was served. It wasn't any good approaching them while they were eating, for North Americans were always bad-tempered when they ate. The best thing to do was stand by their car and when they came out open the door for them. Sometimes they gave him money. Sometimes there were too many people about, selling sandals and serapes, and the North Americans were in a bad temper and just got into their car and drove off fast as if tormented by a swarm of bees.

It was always a matter of mood. The boy knew how to read people's moods and he knew that the fisherman didn't want him to stay on the island, though he knew also that this was the only place that he would be safe from his pursuer.

The boy lived on the outskirts of Colonia Madre in a big concrete culvert which had been lying there for several years. It had been brought there just before an election. Señor Silva, the mayor, had promised that if he were elected he would put a big storm drain under the main road of Colonia Madre so that the road would not be reduced to a swamp during the flash floods of winter. To show how much in earnest he was about this promise he had bought several sections of concrete culvert which had been hauled down from the North American town of San Diego and put on the outskirts of the town.

It had been a great day when these sections of culvert arrived on a huge Yankee truck, lashed to the truck bed with chain. The mayor had made a speech and had written on the side of one of the culverts, in blue paint, the words *el progresso*. Progress—that was his slogan. He had been elected but nothing further had been done about the storm drains and the orphans of the town had soon started living in them, covering the ends with sacking. The boy Juan lived in the one with *el progresso* written on the side in bright blue paint. It was very hot inside during the day and very cold at night, but he could endure these conditions.

The mayor was glad the children lived in the culverts because then he was able to announce that he could not go on with the storm drain project for humanitarian reasons.

"What kind of man would throw these children

compete desperately with the other for money and food. He told some of these about the man who followed him. But since none of the others ever saw the man themselves, none would believe him.

Sometimes, when there was nothing else to do, or if the wind was blowing too hard, Juan went to school in a little mud building at the back of the town. The schoolteacher was Señora Smith. It was a curious name for a Mexican, but her father had been an Englishman or a North American in Mexico City and that was how she had come by it. Although she was not married she was given the title of Señora out of respect for her position. She was as plain as a big adobe brick; a square-set woman who always wore, whatever the temperature, a tweed skirt, fastened around her waist by a broad leather belt, and thick lisle stockings which she mended herself for she had very little money.

She was popularly known around the town as Señora Revolución, for she lived and breathed the great People's Revolution of Mexico and talked of pioneering for the People's Republic. She had been graduated from the university in Mexico City as a teacher, and although she could have obtained much better posts she had deliberately come to Colonia Madre, which was a town of the revolution on the

into the streets to keep water off the road?"
manded in a speech on the subject. "Are we
cans, we citizens of Colonia Madre, to depriv
children of shelter in order to keep mud off o
and our shoes?" The children, providing such
excuse for the mayor, were allowed to stay
they were by the police—who would not have ¡
them anyway. Some of them had been orphans
selves. The mayor obtained the reputation of b
great humanitarian and indeed benefited mo
public opinion than would have been the case h
completed the original project.

A month before he fled to the island Juan had
the short, dark man for the first time. He had
standing outside *el progresso* in the evening whe
boy returned from trying to earn something t
around the town. He looked at Juan, nodded his
and then walked away, but the very look had fri
ened the boy. And then, in the few days before he
fled to the island, every time the boy looked bel
him the short, dark man was there, sometimes
standing and watching him, sometimes following
down a street, sometimes waiting around a cor
when he turned it.

He had a few companions among the other ch
rabble of the town but no real friend, for each had

Mexican frontier of Baja California, to teach the children and to keep alive the doctrine of the revolution. She had been there fifteen years and was as ardent now as on the first day she arrived—an adamant, fighting, fearless, plain-spoken woman who, as Father Sylvester once remarked, was intent on abolishing everything including femininity.

Just before he stole the boat and fled to the Island of the Angels, Juan was in school every day. Surrounded by the others, he knew he was safe from the man who was pursuing him. He had even spoken to the Señora Revolución about the man, but she had said, "You are not getting enough to eat. That is all that is the matter with you. When the revolution matures there will be an end to that." It was no help. The only thing he could do, in his terror, was disappear—and so he had stolen an old flat-bottomed boat and rowed to the Island of the Angels.

Now he was sick and the wind was hissing around the hut and his only comfort was to watch the fisherman sleeping on the floor beside the bed.

"He has gone to sleep facing me," he said. "That is a good sign. If he had turned his back on me there would have been no hope." He was so frightened and desperate that he had to cling to such straws.

## Chapter 5

Francisco had not intended to sleep through the night but it was dawn when he woke. At first he was confused and thought it was only evening, but then he noted that the dim beams of light coming through the cracks of his hut pointed to the west and so were caused by the rising rather than the setting sun. Several times during his sleep he had been conscious of the need to wake up, and once he had been quite sure that he had struggled out of his torpor and had attended to the boy. But now he realized that he had only dreamed this and was dismayed at having slept so long.

The gale was still raging over the island, punctuated by only a few lulls which seemed simply to increase the fury of the wind in the gusts that followed. He and the floor of his hut were covered with a fine desert sand brought over from the mainland by the wind. He got up and went immediately to Juan, who was asleep on the side of the bed, his head turned toward where Francisco had been lying.

There were tear stains on the boy's cheeks; his flesh was hot and grayish and his breath short and very foul-smelling. Plainly the boy was in much worse condition than he had been the day before. Francisco shook him gently. The boy opened his eyes with some difficulty for there was pus at the corners of his eyelids. He turned over on his back. It seemed to Francisco that his neck was swollen.

"How do you feel?" Francisco asked.

"It is hard to breathe," replied Juan.

"Your throat hurts?"

"No."

"Let me take a look at it."

Because of the gloom in the hut caused by the dust

cloud of the gale Francisco had to light an oil lamp to examine the boy's throat. He could not see very well, but there was much more of the gray growth in the throat and here and there were red areas which seemed to be bleeding. Something had to be done, but he had no medical knowledge and for medicine only an old bottle of iodine which had been given to him a year or so before when he had cut his hand badly with a fish knife. The schoolteacher Señora Revolución had given it to him. Although there was no resident doctor in Colonia Madre there was a small dispensary and a doctor visited the town once a month from Ensenada, fifty miles to the north.

With the bottle of iodine the Señora Revolución had given him a child's paint brush and told him to use this to put the iodine on his wound. He found the two now and, having heard something about sterilizing, he boiled a little water and put the brush in it. He was immediately sorry that he had done so, for most of the hairs came off it. They were secured to the handle by a metal ferule, but also glued and the hot water had loosened the glue. Still, he saved enough hair on the brush for his purpose and came back to the boy with it and the bottle.

"Listen," he said. "I am going to put some of this in

your throat. It cures poisons and you have some poison in your throat. But don't swallow it. It will make you gag. But don't mind that. The main thing is don't swallow it. Now open your mouth."

Juan did as he was told; the fisherman dipped the brush in the iodine and inserted the end into the boy's throat. Juan gagged immediately.

"It hurts?"

"Yes."

"Well, we have to do it. Some things hurt but they still have to be done. Afterwards you will feel better."

They tried several times. The first few times the boy gagged, but after a while the nerves of the throat became accustomed to the irritation and Francisco was able to paint the interior liberally with iodine. Then he made some breakfast but all the boy could take was condensed milk with warm water. He had hardly swallowed it before he threw it up and when he put his head back on the bed there was a smear of blood from his nostrils.

"How is the breathing?" asked Francisco, eying the blood and frightened.

"It is better."

"All right. Now listen. I have to get some help. I have to go to Colonia Madre and get some medicine for you. It is morning now. I will be back by the evening—before it is dark."

"The wind . . ." said Juan.

Francisco was suddenly angry. "What about the wind?" he demanded. "Every time the wind blows people are frightened of it. It has been blowing for thousands of years and people are still frightened of it and run into their houses and wring their hands. Well, I am not afraid of the wind. I have been out in the wind many times. I will spit on the wind and I will spit on the wind's mother." He was so enraged that he spat on the floor to show the boy what he thought of the wind. The boy started crying.

"Why are you crying?" demanded Francisco.

"You are angry with me."

"I am not angry with you," stormed Francisco. "I am angry with people who think I am afraid of the wind. Do you think that I, a fisherman, am afraid of the wind?"

"No," said the boy through his tears.

"Well then, I *am* afraid of it," said Francisco surlily. "But I do not want anybody to know about it."

Juan stopped crying and nodded.

"All right," said Francisco. "The sooner I go, the sooner I will be back. Here. I will leave this lamp lit for although I expect to be back before dark, still one never can tell. Oh, don't worry. It is not the sea nor the wind that will delay me but those stupid people in Colonia Madre. Usually they do nothing but talk. They seem to think that talking is doing something. I will leave some water by the bed for you. You had better try to sleep as much of the time as you can." He started to clear up the makeshift bed on the floor. But Juan stopped him.

"Please leave it there," he said.

Francisco looked from the bed to the boy and then shrugged his shoulders in an angry, helpless fashion, though he understood the boy's request. Then he went out of the door into the gale and down the beach to his boat.

The Island of the Angels paralleled the coast of Baja California which ran in a southeasterly direction. Normally, in rowing or sailing to Colonia Madre, which lay directly opposite, Francisco rounded the northwest end of the island to get enough height to compensate for the south-flowing current which carried him out of his way during the crossing. But he decided this time to pass by the southeast end of the island, to stay under its lee for as long as possible and get shelter from the storm which was blowing out of the east.

The hills of the island provided comparatively

smooth water until he left the southeast point; and
then the rollers came snarling down on him, cresting
on their tops and streaked with a wild lace of foam
down their sides. The wind hit with such a blow that
the boat was carried out to sea away from the island
and the mainland for a quarter of a mile before Francisco was able to bring it under control.

He knew the boat well for he had used it for thirty
years and had built it himself. It was heavy, being
very stoutly built, with plenty of buoyancy up forward, its broadest section in the forward half of the
boat. There were three thwarts or seats, one curving
across the transom in the stern, one a third of the
distance forward from the stern, and the other a third
of the distance aft from the bow. The forward seat
had a hole in it through which he stepped his mast,
but he had not brought the mast with him now since
it would have been useless to try to hoist sail in this
kind of weather.

He had been rowing, sitting on the middle seat,
but each time he hit a crest the wind took the bluff
bows of the boat and stopped it dead in the water.
The crests themselves, hissing and roaring down on
him, tried to turn the boat broadside to the waves—
and if that happened it would be capsized. Francisco
waited until the boat was in a deep trough, tempo-

rarily sheltered from the worst of the wind, and then scrambled to the forward seat. He was rowing fiercely before he was properly seated, holding the bow to the creaming water about him. The boat tipped up at such an angle on the back of the wave that he was almost standing when he pulled at the oars. The crest hit the bow square on and the whole boat disappeared in a cascade of spray. Then it started to hurtle down into the next trough and the fisherman rowed desperately to prepare for the crest which would follow in a few seconds.

Near the island the waves were bigger because of the shoaling water and there was a shorter distance between them. But, after forty minutes of struggle, he had got out into deep water and for the first time had a chance to glance at the Island of the Angels and measure his progress. It was much less than he had hoped for. He was, he judged, three miles south of the island but hardly a quarter of a mile closer to the mainland. It would take him, then, twenty hours or more to reach the mainland and he had not the strength for such a struggle. There was no hope of reaching Colonia Madre directly. He would have to land perhaps twenty miles down the coast and then walk to the town.

It did not occur to him that he might not have the strength to walk twenty miles after struggling for several hours in the boat against the rioting wind and sea. Had such a thought occurred to him he would have dismissed it with impatience. It was not a matter of what he had the strength to do, but of what had to be done. He had to get to Colonia Madre and he would find the strength somewhere.

He eased the boat a little to the south to take advantage of the current, watching the crests behind him all the while, and settled down to his rowing. He made his best speed in the troughs, using only enough strength on the crests to keep the boat headed into them. In an hour he was soaked through and there was a lot of water in the bottom of the boat. He tucked the bailing pan between his feet and when the water, slushing around in the boat, filled or half-filled it, he stopped quickly, hardly interrupting his rowing, and threw the water overboard. It was an old trick and one which had served him many times in the past.

When he had left the island he had felt frightened by the wildness of wind and water but now his self-confidence began to return. "I am a fisherman," he said. "That is not something to be put aside." He tried not to think of the boy lying in the hut because, when he did so, his self-confidence ebbed and he felt a twinge of desperation and fear.

There were two lives at stake—his own and the boy's. The boy's life depended on him. That was what made him afraid. He had never carried such a burden before.

## Chapter 6

It was the middle of the afternoon before Francisco reached the mainland. He came ashore on a wild beach across which the sand was streaming like swiftly moving mist. It stung his face and his hands and his bare feet and he had to bend his head down to breathe. The last three miles of his journey had not been bad, however, because the coastal water lay in the lee of the land and, although streaked with foam, there was not enough fetch for the waves to build up.

The whole shore where the water touched the beach was crowded thick with tumbleweed, great balls of it torn from the desert and bobbing about in the water. He had to get through fifty feet of this thicket of desert growth now floating on the sea to reach the sand and haul his boat up beyond the reach of the tide. He stopped long enough to hide the oars and to pull the bung out of the bottom so the boat would drain. He put the bung in the pocket of his ragged trousers and then headed inland to where he knew there was a road leading to Colonia Madre in the northwest.

This road ran through the terrible deserts of Baja California to La Paz in the tropical south of the peninsula. It was proudly called Highway Number One, but it was indeed the only highway which ran the length of the peninsula. In this part it was not paved, being nothing more than a track down which trucks traveled between Tijuana and Ensenada in the north and La Paz. The distance was several hundred miles with only a few ranch houses in between. Francisco judged that he must be about twenty miles south of Colonia Madre; his best chance of getting there was to find the road and hope he would be picked up by a truck. Though whether a truck would be traveling in the gale was extremely doubtful.

The distance from the beach to the road was almost two miles across mountainous desert, for the road lay behind a coastal fringe of mountains, and it was close to five o'clock when Francisco finally reached the road. Here the wind was not quite so wild, being held off by the mountains around, though it roared down the valleys at times, carrying desert debris with it.

When he got to the road, Francisco squatted down on his heels for a while. He was tired and thirsty. His clothes, caked with salt from the sea water which the wind had dried, were now also caked with dust. His hair was covered with it, his scruffy beard, his hands and his feet. He resembled not so much a man as some tattered animal which, like a man, walked upright. He put his head between his hands, screwed his eyes tightly shut, which was his way of resting, stood up and started walking northward along the road. The dust and salt caked on his clothing made his trousers heavy and they pulled down around his waist where they were fastened with a piece of rope.

After a little while the rope started to chafe his hips and the flesh smarted. But this was nothing about which he could do anything and so he endured it. Then he started counting, which was a favorite method with him of enduring things. He first counted his steps, but the numbers ran higher than his head could contain. So he started counting the number of barrel cactus that he passed growing on the left-hand side of the road. First of all he counted them all, even those that were diseased or dead, but after a while he decided to count the live ones only.

"Whoever bothers to count the dead?" he asked himself. "It is impossible and worthless to make a count of dead things."

Once he glanced behind him in the swirling dust at a large barrel cactus which was distorted on one side though still alive. He stopped walking to look at it, a hundred feet to his rear, and a dust devil swept up the road and enveloped it. Then he thought he was a man standing in the road, but decided that he had mistaken the shape of the cactus in the whirling dust for a man and went on. After that, however, he glanced behind him more often and several times thought he saw a man, a short, dark man as the boy had described. He was always to the side of the road, standing and looking at him.

"I am beginning to believe the boy's tale," he said. "It is surely nothing but a cactus and the dust."

The sun had set shortly after he reached the road behind the mountain, but, since it had not gone behind the horizon but was only shadowed by the mountain peaks, it was still light. But after two hours of walking it was dusk and would soon be dark. Since there was not likely to be either starlight or moonlight which could penetrate the dustcloud, he decided, while a little light yet remained, to walk in the center of the road, for it would be easy to stray off it if he kept to one side.

He could not count anything anymore other than his footsteps and he tried to think of some other method of enduring his situation. He grew tired. He squatted in the road and started to tremble from sheer exhaustion and cold, for, with the disappearance of the sun, the temperature had dropped thirty degrees. His chest hurt him from sucking in the dirt-laden air through his teeth.

"I must start walking again," he said, but not a single nerve or muscle in his body responded to the statement. "I must get up and walk again," he repeated, and this time he made an effort to get up; but, although he willed the muscles of his legs to move, they would not respond or, rather, they responded with so little strength that he could not raise himself from his squatting position. His chest hurt more when he made the effort.

"The boy," he said, and the picture of the boy lying alone in the hut with a smear of blood from his nose was so vivid that he cried out and, putting one hand on the ground, pushed himself upright, though he had to use his hands on his legs to straighten his torso. When he was upright he saw the stranger again, an indistinct figure in the gloom.

"Go away," he cried. "I am not the boy. I am not to be frightened by you." But he was frightened nonetheless. Then there was a roar above the hissing of the wind from down the road and the golden headlights of a truck swung through the dust toward him. The truck stopped with a great shuddering of its overloaded chassis but Francisco could not see past the headlights. He stumbled around to the door of the driver's cab and the driver opened for him.

"What in the name of the devil are you doing in this wind sitting down in the middle of the road? I could have run over you like a rabbit," said the driver.

"I am going to get help for the boy," Francisco

said. The problem had been with him so deeply and for so long that he assumed that everybody must know what boy he was talking about. "Colonia Madre," he added and then he fell asleep.

On the island Juan spent most of the day awake, watching the bed where Francisco had lain and watching also the shafts of light moving across the floor as the sun journeyed west. He never got accustomed to the hissing and booming of the wind and dreaded even more the lulls, which he knew would be followed by renewed furies. He knew that the fisherman would not be back by nightfall. He had been able to tell that from Francisco's face when he left.

As the day wore on he began to be troubled as to whether Francisco would get back at all, or whether he would be drowned in attempting the crossing. In desperation he tried to fight this thought down but it kept recurring. He pondered whether he should put out the oil lamp to save the oil for when night came. It took a great deal of courage to turn out the lamp, which had been put in a fish box by his bed with a box of matches, but he did so. When the lamp was out he had a feeling that he would never see Fran-

cisco again, for the flame of the lamp was a sort of bond between them and now it was extinguished. He had to fight that idea down too.

Toward evening he lit the lamp again and then he felt better and, for the first time since the fisherman left the island, he fell asleep.

## Chapter 7

The Señora Revolución lived in a clapboard house about two hundreds yards up a dirt road from the school, which itself was in the back part of the town of Colonia Madre. Her house was the only one in the town that was painted every year. She painted it herself. To do so was part of the spirit of the revolution which she preached. A prime doctrine of the revolution was that people's surroundings had a great effect on them, and to improve people you had to improve their surroundings. So she kept her house painted and she also had a garden laid out in which she grew corn, lettuce and beans. In truth, she needed to grow these vegetables and any others she could get to survive in the clay soil for her salary was hardly enough to feed her, let alone keep her decently clothed.

She grew no flowers, for flowers could not be eaten and they were a luxury which the people could not afford. Later, when the revolution had matured—she always spoke of its maturing rather than succeeding —there would be time for flowers and other luxuries for the people. That would be taken care of. Meantime, the pressing needs were good housing, food and education.

She always put in a very long day, rising at six in the morning and rarely getting to bed until midnight. After she had dressed, she made her bed, watered her garden, got together her schoolwork, drank a cup of very hot coffee and spent half an hour at the dispensary before going to her school at eight-thirty. The school embraced every grade from children of six to boys and girls of fourteen—if any could be persuaded to attend that long. All had to be taught in one classroom, divided from each other by invisible walls of learning.

She taught reading, writing and arithmetic and the history of Mexico, which always became the history of the revolution. She permitted no religious teaching in the school and no pictures or statues of religious significance. This made her the arch enemy of Father Sylvester, who thought of the Señora Revolución in terms of Lucifer. While she lectured about the practical materialism of the revolution, he preached about the godless influence which was taking hold of the minds of the children of the town of Colonia Madre.

Caught between these two forces, those of the children of the town who attended both school and church took refuge in a world of their own which was a compromise between the two opposing camps. God would take care of them in the church and the Señora Revolución could take care of them in the school. If one failed, the other was sure to help.

The school closed for the siesta from noon to three o'clock, but the schoolteacher hated the siesta as much as she hated Sunday Mass. It was a degeneracy against which she fought valiantly but without avail. She, herself, refusing both church and siesta, went home for lunch and then visited anyone around the town who was sick until three when the school

opened again. It closed at six. There was an hour of
work at the dispensary, then dinner, and then school
work, reading and so on until midnight when the
Señora Revolución went to bed.

Buffeted in her daily round the day the gale
started, she had gone to bed especially tired that
night. She owned a transistor radio and, tuning in to
the eleven o'clock broadcast before retiring, had
heard that a center of low pressure was situated three
hundred miles off the coast and was moving slowly
inland. The gale would last for several days. There
would be a week of wind and dust whirling over the
countryside, ruining crops, damaging houses, causing
deaths and sickness, undoing all the patient toil and
planning of the people. If she had not long ago become master of her emotions, which had no part in
the revolution, she would have wept over it—wept
over the fury that swept Mexico, wept over the im-
potence of men in the face of the elements, wept over
the destruction of her own garden in which not a
thing would have survived when the wind was gone.

Before she went to sleep she recalled that Father
Sylvester had held a special benediction at the
church that evening, with prayers for the abatement
of the gale, and more people had gone to the service

than attended her school. Even her best pupil, a
sixteen-year-old boy whom she was planning to get
sent to the university in Mexico City and who was
full of the pioneering spirit of the revolution, had
gone to the service. Well, they were all weak but she
was a rock and neither wind, dust, nor the mumbled
Latin prayers of the priest would move her. She
would endure them all. With this thought she went
to sleep, leaving the oil lamp burning low on the
table in the living room.

She was awakened about two o'clock in the morning by the headlights of a truck shining through her
bedroom window and somebody thundering on her
front door. She wore a long flannel nightgown and
with her iron-gray hair tumbling around her shoulders, turned up the oil lamp and opened the door.
Two men stumbled in and helped her to shut it
against the velocity of the wind. One looked as
though he were made of clay, or as if he had been
buried in a grave of clay and monstrously resur-
rected. His eyes, nostrils and mouth were mere holes
in a mask of dirt that covered his face, and his clothes
were coated with the same dirt. The other was in
better condition and a much bigger man. He wore a
leather jacket and was plainly the driver of the truck.

"You have to help me, Señora Revolución," said the smaller man. "I am Francisco the fisherman. There is a boy on my island and he is dying. You must help me right away."

She stared at him. She knew her people well. Any sickness, particularly if it occurred at night, seemed to them fatal and this man was obviously hysterical.

"How do you know he is dying?" she asked.

"Great heaven," cried Francisco. "What a question! A man of my years knows when someone is dying. There is blood coming from his nose. He can hardly breathe. His throat is full of poison."

"Calm yourself," said the schoolteacher. "There is blood coming from his nose. Did he fall?"

"No," cried the fisherman. "He was nearly drowned. I found him lying outside my door when I came in with the two grouper." And then he realized that it was hopeless to continue in this way and he stopped.

"Believe me, Señora," he said, "the boy is dying. If you do not come to the island with some medicine to help him, he will die."

"I cannot help you until you tell me quietly what is the matter with this boy. Calm yourself and tell me what is the matter with him."

Francisco made a great effort and told her about
the boy. He was not accustomed to having long con-
versations with other people and to organizing his
thoughts in order to convey his point. He told everything he knew about the boy, about his being chased
by the stranger, about him coming ashore in a boat
which could not be found, about his throat and the
blood and how he had come to the mainland to get
help. In the end the schoolteacher concluded that
there was a sick boy on the island, that the fisherman,
left alone with him, had become quite hysterical and
had very foolishly left the boy alone. In any case,
since with the gale still raging it was quite impossible
to think of going to the island, she advised him that
the best thing to do was to wait until daylight when
he would have rested and she would be able to think
about what could be done

The truck driver, who had remained quiet up to
this point, agreed with the schoolteacher. "In these
cases it is sometimes better to do nothing at all," he
said. "There is no sense running around the place like
a cockerel with its head chopped off."

For a while Francisco could not believe that they
were not going to help him. "I have come all this
way," he said. "I have been eight hours in my boat

and I have been six hours getting here. Can you tell me that I have come here senselessly as if I had my head chopped off?"

"No," said the truck driver. "Nonetheless, you would perhaps have done better to stay on the island."

"Don't you understand that he is dying and that somebody has to help him?" Francisco demanded. He stiffened for a moment and closed his eyes for the pain from his tiredness and breathing the dust was excruciating in his chest and arms. It even reached up into the muscles of his neck and his jaws. For a little while he was conscious of nothing but the pain and then it went away and the relief was immense.

"There is something the matter with you?" the schoolteacher asked, eying him sharply.

"It is nothing. Just the dust and I am tired."

"Well," said the truck driver. "I will have to go. I have to be at Ensenada tomorrow afternoon and I must sleep." He turned to the fisherman. "Don't walk in the middle of the road," he said. "You could have been killed." He gave a little bow to the schoolteacher, pulled the door open and wrestled it shut himself from the outside.

"Señora," said the fisherman, "I beg you to believe

me. The boy is alone. He can scarcely breathe because his throat is so bad. You must come with some
medicine and help him."

"Describe to me again the condition of his throat,"
said the schoolteacher and the fisherman did. It was
only then that the schoolteacher realized that the boy
had diphtheria.

She had some years before bought from an American publisher, on the installment plan, a volume
called *The Home Physician*. It was her medical text,
but useful only in making a diagnosis, for at the end
of each diagnosis there were always the words,
"Treatment. Keep the patient comfortable and call a
physician." It was of course precisely at this point
that she needed advice and the book offered none.
Still the diagnosis was helpful. She took the volume,
looked up diphtheria and read the description and
symptoms, and the symptoms matched almost too
precisely what the fisherman had told her.

Well, the prognosis was death—either death from
suffocation when the membrane that formed in the
throat closed up the air passage, or death from a general weakness of the body. Treatment? There
was mention of an antitoxin but no such remedy was
available to her. The nearest source of supply was

Ensenada. There was a doctor at the hospital there who had given her his number to call in case of an emergency. It was he who had insisted that a telephone be installed in her house and she reached for it now. It was the kind that had a handle which had to be cranked to call the operator. She cranked and cranked again without result. Plainly the line had been blown down by the wind.

She replaced the receiver and said, "It is hopeless. There is nothing I can do."

Immediately Francisco was angry and in his anger he forgot the respect that was due to the schoolteacher. "What do you mean there is nothing you can do?" he cried. "You turn that thing there and put it down and say there is nothing you can do when I have come all this way. Do you think I have come here to see you turn that handle and have you tell me when it fails that you can do nothing? This is a child who is dying. Does that handle there tell you that it won't work and so the child must die? Are you a woman, a human being, or just something that turns handles and takes whatever answer they give you?"

"You have no right to talk to me like that," said the schoolteacher, stung to anger herself.

"Never mind what rights I have," said Francisco.

"Give me some medicine and tell me what to do with it and I will take it to the boy myself."

"You could kill the boy with medicines that you do not understand," said the schoolteacher. "Take my advice and go to sleep and we will think what to do in the morning."

"Death will not wait until the morning," said Francisco. "Give me at least a new brush to put the iodine on his throat." He had told her about this treatment.

She shrugged and went to a cabinet containing bottles and bandages and brought back a brush and a tongue depressor whose use she explained to him.

Francisco stuffed them in his pocket, opened the door and went out. He tried to shut it against the wind but he had not the strength and the schoolteacher had to close it herself from the inside. She stood looking at the door when it was closed and said bitterly, "When the revolution matures, such things will not happen. We will have doctors for the people."

A second later a terrible rage overtook her. The wind and the dust and all her struggles and frustrations and work overwhelmed her and she picked up the useless telephone and smashed it on the floor. "Revolution!" she shouted. "Revolution! Who cares about revolution? It is too late for it. We have only ourselves." She wrenched the door open and ran out into the wind in her flannel nightdress which billowed behind her like a sail.

"Wait for me, fisherman!" she shouted. "Wait for me! I will come now and help you."

## Chapter 8

When he left the schoolteacher's house, the truck
driver had headed his truck up the road again for
Ensenada. The dust was so bad that he had to use his
windshield wipers to see through the windshield and
he had several times debated just pulling the truck to
the side and going to sleep. But he was a man who,
once he had made up his mind to do one thing, became convinced a few seconds later that that was not
the right course to follow. All his life he had lived in

this kind of indecision or, rather, of decisions made only to be reversed and then reversed again. He had no wisdom. That was his trouble and it had been his trouble since boyhood. Only his wife was able to make up his mind for him for any length of time, and when he was with her he was at peace. She decided everything that was to be done and he did it. But, now that he was alone in his truck, these problems of decision were thrust solely upon him and he had to decide whether he should stop and sleep a little in the truck or whether he should push on to Ensenada, where there was a bed in a lodging house where he could sleep with a clear conscience, his work done.

"Certainly this is doing the truck no good," he said to himself, debating the problem of whether to proceed or stop. "The dust is choking the air filter. The carburetors are not getting enough air. The engine will flood and then I will be forced to stop. Better to stop now and sleep. Perhaps by daylight the wind will have died down."

This argument appeared to him to be soundly based, and he was about to pull over to the side of the road and switch off the engine when it occurred to him that there was no certainty at all that the gale would end with daylight. It might continue. If it continued he would be faced with the same problem and, added to that, he would be late in getting to Ensenada and, added to that, he would not have slept well in the truck. On top of this, because he would be late arriving in Ensenada, he might be expected to take another truck back right away without any proper rest.

"The devil with it," he said. "Obviously I must continue driving." But the engine coughed a few minutes later and he started going over the whole problem again. He was still uncertain what to do as he left Colonia Madre and spotted in his headlights the church and the priest's house next to it. He started to turn the corner out of the town. There was a light in the priest's house and he immediately decided to stop there. He would stop there and tell the priest about the sick boy on the island, and in so doing he might be able to get from the priest some advice as to whether to continue his journey or not. Whatever the priest said, that was what he would do. A priest would certainly not tell him wrong.

So he pulled up by the priest's house and knocked on the door and after a few moments Father Sylvester opened it. He was a huge man and filled the doorway. He was angry and hissed, "What is it?" and then pulled the truck driver inside and shut the door against the wind.

The truck driver, nervous as he was at disturbing the priest, nonetheless could not help but admire the priest's strength in shutting the door merely by putting his huge shoulder against it.

"Well," said Father Sylvester. "What do you want?"

"Excuse me for disturbing you, Father," said the truck driver. "But there is a boy dying."

"Where?"

"On the Island of the Angels."

"How do you know?"

The truck driver explained how he knew.

"And where is this fisherman now?" asked the priest when the truck driver had finished his story.

"I left him at Señora Revolución's while I came here to tell you," replied the truck driver. This was by no means the truth. He had had no intention whatever of telling the priest, but had come only to see if he could get some advice or comfort about driving his truck.

"The Señora Revolución," snapped the priest. "Why didn't he come to me first? It is a strange world when an atheist and a priest are summoned to the same bedside. One would think that people could make up their minds about such matters . . . make a choice. One or the other."

. "He went to the Señora Revolución to get some medical help," said the truck driver, looking at the floor and wondering how it was that he should feel guilty since he had done nothing in the matter but pick up the fisherman.

"Hah," said the priest. "And is she going to the island in this gale with him?"

"I do not think so," said the truck driver. "In fact, I do not believe she will."

"That's it!" cried the priest. "That is your revolution for you. That is your great People's Revolution. Mass meetings, programs, solidarity, pamphlets, organization—everything for The People but nothing for one individual. But God made individuals, not people. When he felt like making what the Señora Revolución calls The People he made sheep. She should preach her revolution to sheep but not to individual creations of God."

"Yes, Father," said the truck driver.

"She is too stupid to know this," continued the priest.

"That is true," said the truck driver. "I went to

confession last Friday," he added, for he felt that he
was somehow being identified with the Señora Revolución, and he wanted to assure the priest that he
was a good Catholic himself.

"Tell me what you know of the boy's sickness,"
said the priest, still angry. But he always spoke in an
angry fashion for there were many things that angered him. His own size angered him. It made him
look as if, in a hungry parish, he was the only
one who ate three square meals a day. In fact he ate
very little, yet everything he ate turned to bone and
muscle and strength. He had often prayed for some
sickness that would reduce him to a skeleton for the
rest of his life so that his size would not scandalize
his parishioners. But no such miracle had been
vouchsafed him.

The truck driver told him what he knew of the
condition of the boy, and Father Sylvester, who had
attended the deaths of most of the people in Colonia
Madre for ten years and had become quite a good
diagnostician as a result, guessed at diphtheria.

"The Señora Revolución must be made to go to
the boy," he said, completely reversing his previous
stand about an atheist and a priest being at a
deathbed. "I will rub her nose in her stupid revolu-

tion and make her realize the importance of an individual. . . ."

"Yes," said the truck driver. He added, greatly daring, "However, she has attended many sick people before."

"Propaganda," snapped the priest. "This takes courage."

"Father," said the truck driver, realizing that his own problem was not yet solved, "I need some advice. Do you think I should go to Ensenada?"

"You will not go anywhere except to the house of the Mayor and tell him to give you the keys of that big boat of his, and bring them to me at the house of the Señora Revolución."

"But if he will not give me the keys?"

"If he will not give you the keys, tell him I will not fail to mention the fact in my sermon next Sunday. Mother Church should not interfere in politics, but Mother Church has a duty to denounce publicly any disgraceful behavior in those elected to look after the welfare of the public. Tell him that and tell him I wish him good night."

"And about Ensenada . . ."

"What about Ensenada?"

"When I have brought you the keys should I take my truck through the gale to Ensenada?"

"If that is your duty, that is what you should do."

"But the dust may get into the engine . . ."

"Then pray," snapped the priest. "Do your duty and pray. It is the only thing you can do since you seem incapable of using your head." With that he picked up a worn tin box which contained all needed for the administration of the sacrament of extreme unction and hurled himself through the door, out into the gale—as violent himself, it seemed to the truck driver, as the wind that plucked at his flying cassock and the blanket he had thrown over his shoulders.

The priest went immediately to the house of the Señora Revolución. He banged on the door and then pushed it open and found her preparing a case of medicines. The fisherman was in a chair asleep. The Señora Revolución's hair was still streaming down her back but she had gathered it together with a ribbon. Perhaps it was this that made her seem less formidable, less like iron, to the priest.

"They told me you would not come," said the priest.

She nodded her head toward Francisco, lying in his filthy clothes in the chair. "I, too, am a Mexican," she said, and to the priest it sounded as though there was a touch of pity in her voice. He had never known her to show pity and he was amazed and for the first time since he had come to Colonia Madre some of his own anger left him.

## Chapter 9

Father Sylvester took the wheel of the Mayor's cabin cruiser to go over to the Island of the Angels. He was familiar with the controls, for he had several times been invited to go fishing with the Mayor, usually when the Mayor had come up for election or when other political events were pending in which he felt that the priest's influence would be beneficial. This was a torment to the priest, who loved fishing but hated to be used as a political tool and who many times stated vehemently that it was no part of the function of Mother Church to interfere in political matters. Still, the temptation to go fishing was always strong, and there was the argument that he could give his catch (usually a good one) to the poorer people of the parish. And the Mayor always assured him that no politics would be discussed, though he had a sliding kind of way of bringing up political discussion disguised as charitable work on which the priest should be consulted anyway.

Father Sylvester liked things to be either black or white—God or devil—and he was always angered at the Mayor's method of mixing up Christian charity and political jobbery. This was one of the main things, including his own size, that kept him in a continuous state of anger and he had once warned the Mayor vehemently that men did not jump into Hell but that they slipped in there while persuading themselves that they were traveling in the other direction.

"Ah, well," the Mayor had replied, "there is always God's grace," and this had angered the priest even further, for he looked upon God's grace as something for emergency use only and not something easily obtained by holding out a fat hand—spiritually speaking—and saying "Please."

Although he was familiar with the controls of the
cruiser, he had never taken it out in the kind of
weather which he now had to face. For a little distance off the shore the sea was flat, though laced with
foam. But a half mile offshore the waves started to
build, cresting horribly in the dark behind the
cruiser, flinging her big stern up in the air, launching
her forward until her nose started to bury in the
trough of the wave ahead, which she was at times in
danger of overtaking, the wave then, at last, passing
underneath her, to repeat the ordeal over and over
again.

The priest was enough of a seaman to shut down
the throttle when he felt the stern rise on a big wave.
This cut the cruiser's speed and let the wave pass
under her, but he still experienced some terrible
sleigh rides when boat and wave kept pace. At such
times his rudder was useless, for, since the cruiser
was moving at the same speed as the water, the rudder had no effect. He would throttle back desperately, hoping that the cruiser would not broach to. If
she did, she would be turned over in the water and
they would all be drowned.

Several times in the first half-hour he thought of
waking Francisco, who had been ordered to lie down,
dirty clothes and all, in the Mayor's beautiful double

bunk below. Francisco, to be sure, knew nothing of
how to handle a power boat, but he had a thorough
knowledge of the sea in all its conditions. Eventually,
after the cruiser had been caught on the foaming
crest of one especially large rogue wave and flung
forward for four hundred yards like a javelin until her
bow was buried in the dark sea, he shouted to the
Señora Revolución to get the fisherman up. Francisco woke immediately, perhaps sensing, even in his
torpor, that something was amiss and, without even
rubbing the sleep out of his eyes, he summed up the
situation.

"Slow it down," he shouted to the priest, above the
hissing of the sea and the shriek of the wind.

The priest indicated that the boat was slowed as
much as was possible. Francisco started pulling open
lockers in the cockpit like a madman and finally
found a thick Dacron line. He found the two ends,
fastened them to cleats on each side of the cruiser
and without waiting to unroll the line seized the rest
of it and threw it over the stern. The effect was close
to miraculous. The line snaked out in the water to
form a big loop behind the boat. The crests that were
following and then overtaking them disappeared, and
the cruiser immediately started to answer her helm
though the control was still precarious.

In his fumbling Francisco came across a cone-shaped piece of canvas, the wider end held open by a hoop of stainless steel. It was a sea anchor or drogue. He had never seen such a contrivance before but he guessed at its use from his knowledge of the sea. He tied a bowline onto a bridle in the hoop with another piece of line and tied the end of the line to a cleat. Then he threw the cone overboard. It snaked away into the dark water and the line snapped tight with a twang that could be heard even above the wind. The cruiser seemed to stop in the water. Wave after wave roared down on her, lifted up her broad stern, passed under and went on with a mutter as if grumbling at being cheated of its prey.

All this had been the work of only a few minutes. In that time the fisherman had been drenched with spray. He climbed up to the flying bridge where the priest had the wheel, and the priest saw in the light from the control panel that Francisco's face was washed clean of the mud. It was as if he had been raised from the dead.

The fisherman looked at the controls but they meant nothing to him; and all the green-glowing dials measuring oil pressure, engine temperature, revolutions of the port and starboard engines, and the amount of current that was entering the batteries frightened him. He was sure that if he touched anything he would ruin some part of this delicate and complicated boat. But he had to take the wheel.

He knew boats and he knew that this boat was not being properly handled. It felt uneasy under him and the feeling of uneasiness permeated every fiber of his body. The priest gave him the wheel, glad to be relieved of the responsibility for the cruiser, and demonstrated the accelerator and indicated the compass. He had been steering a course of 270 degrees—due west—which was the direction in which the Island of the Angels lay from the harbor of Colonia Madre.

But the fisherman, though he knew what a compass was, did not trust it. He pushed the accelerator forward and heard and felt the propellers start to bite in the water. The cruiser, pulling the terrible weight of the drogue and the warp which he had put under the stern, settled a little but still strove forward. Francisco looked around at the sky. It was full of racing clouds and of dust, though the dust was not so bad out to sea as it had been over the land.

He was looking for a star, any star, which he could recognize, however briefly seen. If he could catch a glimpse of one, he would know where he was and in what direction the island lay in the howling darkness ahead of him. The clouds remained covering the heavens, and the priest was horrified to see the compass card swing until the lubberline pointed to 270 and then to 280 and then to 290 degrees. On this course the cruiser was taking the waves on her starboard quarter and the motion was greatly aggravated. He pointed to the compass, jerking his forefinger down at it as if to stab it through the hemisphere of glass which encased it, but Francisco shook his head and kept the boat at 290 degrees though he was not watching the compass card.

Without a star, he was steering by the waves— knowing that the current ran to the southward and the wind was from the east. The waves then would be running roughly southeast and the current taking the boat with them. To steer the right course he had to take the seas on his quarter. He could not plot this on paper nor explain it to anyone, but he knew that that was what he had to do.

With the waves on his quarter, he might clear the southeast end of the island. It would be best to come around that way. He would get under the lee quicker. He would also have a better chance of clawing off if the island suddenly appeared out of the dark wilderness which ended in an obscurity of nothing a hundred feet ahead.

At last he saw a star, saw two close together and tilted toward the north. He knew them immediately. They were old friends, lighthouses that had guided him back many times to the island. From their position in the sky he knew it was about three o'clock in the morning and that the island lay ahead of him but a little to the west. He pointed them out to the priest and smiled. One star was missing from the group, but it soon appeared, making a line of three—the belt of Orion.

He moved the accelerator forward, swung the polished wheel a little to the right, and stared ahead looking for breakers. He saw them long before the priest did, columns of roaring water flung high into the air and then roaring away to leeward so that they made a long streak of white on the brooding ocean. When the priest saw them he was frightened but Francisco was still smiling. He brought the cruiser just outside the end of the line of spray, gunned the throttle, put the helm over. In a few minutes they were under the lee of the Island of the Angels, still with the drogue and the warp over the stern, but moving toward the bay where the fisherman's hut stood.

The fisherman kept looking ashore to see a light from his hut—but even when he knew he was close into the bay and it was time to get the priest to anchor the cruiser, he could not see it.

Then at last he saw it, a mere glow which brightened and then darkened in the slipstream of the dust from the desert and the hills of the island.

There was a dinghy lashed to the foredeck of the cruiser and he had it in the water before the priest had finished with the anchor. He hustled both of his passengers in, storming at the priest who went below to get a powerful spotlight which was aboard the cruiser. Then the fisherman pulled the dinghy ashore.

When they got out, he seized the dinghy by the breasthook and singlehandedly wrenched it up the beach, and then ran to the hut. He got there before either of them and threw open the door and cried, "Boy! You see! I have come back! Everything is going to be all right."

On the bed, the boy did not even turn his head toward him.

## Chapter 10

The boy was not dead, but in a stupor compounded of weakness and of fear. He feared that the fisherman had either deserted him or been drowned and that therefore he must die. Every time he had waked during the night he had faced this fear; at last it had been more than he could bear and he had retreated in his terror into the shadow of death. At least that was the way the Señora Revolución explained the matter; though the priest said it was a mortal sin to will one's self into death in this manner, and he would not believe it.

The Señora Revolución did not waste any time when she got to the hut. She pushed the fisherman aside and took the boy's wrist and felt for a pulse. It was there, tiny, very quick, but still there. So he was alive. Next she took his head, bent it to one side, and opened his mouth. The priest shined the spotlight into it, and she depressed the tongue and saw that the gray membrane covered most of the back of the throat. There were bloody spots in some places where he had coughed it away. She opened a wooden box with a rough cross marked in red on it, pulled out a tube and to the fisherman's amazement put it down the boy's throat. Then she sucked at the end of the tube, producing a gurgling sound and tearing away the membrane which threatened to clog the throat completely. She then blew out what was in the tube, going to the door of the hut to do so, and repeated the process.

The priest watched her stonily. He knew that what she was doing could kill her; for if the membrane got into her own throat, or even if the bacillus lodged in her breathing passages, she herself could catch diphtheria. He admired her but he was no sentimentalist.

He knew himself that this was what had to be done and if she had not done it, then he would have done it himself. When she had finished with this operation, she took a bent aluminum tube and put it down the boy's throat, forcing it down the windpipe. She sucked on this to be sure that it was clear and then, satisfied, left it there. The fisherman could hear the air whistling down the tube and out again from the boy's lungs.

"Well, she is a brave one," said the priest to himself. "I have seen doctors who blew down the tube to force the infection into the patient's lungs rather than risk sucking it into their own."

Satisfied that the boy was able to breathe, the Señora Revolución opened her white box with the red cross on it and took out an old syringe and an ampule of penicillin.

She looked at it and shrugged. "I don't think it will touch diphtheria," she said, "but there may be something else here. In any case it will not hurt." She filled the syringe, examined the boy's bony shoulder, and shook her head.

"No more meat than a sparrow," she declared, rolled him over and put the needle into his thin buttocks.

"How much?" asked the priest, for he felt that he might be consulted in these medical matters.

"Enough for a horse," said the Señora Revolución. "Yes, even enough for you. Well. That is all I can do. You try now."

"You are mistaken," said the priest angrily. "It is not what you can do or what I can do but what God can do. That is the whole thing in a nutshell."

"It was the Englishman Fleming who developed penicillin."

"It was God who invented the Englishman Fleming," said the priest. "In any case he did not come out of the dogma of your revolution."

"Be quiet," said the fisherman. "Why are you always arguing? It doesn't matter to the boy. All that matters to him is his next breath."

The priest looked at the boy and then at the Señora Revolución. "I am going to administer a sacrament," he said angrily. "I ask you, even if you do not believe in this sacrament, to be quiet. If you can bring yourself to do so, kneel down. It is called the last sacrament of my church, but it is not a sacrament of death but of healing. It is the laying on of hands and the anointing with oil and a cry to God to spare a life if that be his will. Perhaps you can kneel for that—in pity, if not in reverence."

He put the band of cloth—the stole—around his
neck and the fisherman knelt immediately. He bowed
down until his head was almost touching the floor
and he put his face in his hands. If the boy was to be
saved, God would do it. God would come down to
the boy's bed and touch the boy through the hands of
the priest. He was afraid of such a thing happening,
but with every ounce of energy he had left he prayed
that it would happen. He prayed until his heart and
his mind seemed to be fused together in one thrusting
force that reached up to heaven, and there was one
brief second in his tremendous prayer when he felt
that everything would be all right and the boy would
live.

The Señora Revolución looked at him with con-
tempt. There he was and there was Mexico—soiled,
hungry, dirty, ignorant, beaten to the ground, and
groveling in the presence of some superstition. Then
the fisherman raised his head and looked at her and
she saw his face for the first time, cleared of the clay.
In the harsh lines and the flat brow and the stubbled
chin and thin mouth was an eternity of courage and
of endurance, and in the eyes, which were red-
rimmed from utter weariness, there was hope as in
the eyes of a child. At the sight of that she knelt. The

priest turned, having administered the sacrament and saw the schoolteacher kneeling. He was about to say something but she cut him off.

"For my people," she said. "Not for you. For those." And she nodded at the fisherman.

"You had better find some place to sleep," the priest said. "I will watch him. We have both done all we can." Immediately, he corrected himself and said, "I mean we have done what God has permitted us to do to the best of our knowledge and it rests now with His will."

"You are a Dominican," said the Señora Revolución. "A Jesuit could split the hair even finer. I know. I have argued with them." But she smiled when she said this. The priest suspected that she was teasing him and, surprised, he smiled back at her.

It was a week before the boy was past the crisis and another week before he could be moved from the island to Colonia Madre, there to be taken to a hospital in Ensenada, a matter which the schoolteacher had arranged with her doctor friend. She explained to the boy that though he was well he was still in an infectious state and might give the disease to others. He would have to stay in the hospital until the doctor was assured that none of the bacillus remained in his throat or his breathing passages.

The fisherman went to Colonia Madre with the boy but would not go to Ensenada since he did not like cities. He told the boy that when he came back he could come and live with him on the island and the boy knew, looking at the fisherman's face, that he meant this and he was content and happy.

There was a great deal of fuss made in Colonia Madre about the saving of the boy, but in some subtle way the fisherman received little credit and was commonly reckoned to have acted rather stupidly in the matter. Several people were able to point out that they would have acted more cleverly and not allowed so much time to be wasted. And the Mayor got great credit for having placed his fine cabin cruiser at the disposal of the priest and the Señora Revolución and so really saving the boy's life.

The Mayor was very pleased about this and not entirely innocent of encouraging the report which brought him the credit, for there was another election coming up. But the Señora Revolución interviewed him alone in his office and told him that there had to be a doctor in Colonia Madre and he had better see that there was one because if there wasn't she and the priest would combine against him. Faced with this unexpected combination, the Mayor promised he would get a doctor—and one was brought to the town.

As for the fisherman, he was first of all concerned about the boat which he had built with his own hands. He walked back to the place where he had left it, for no one, not even the Mayor, offered him a ride. He found the boat on the beach and, although it was almost full of sand blown in by the wind, it was in good condition. He emptied the sand out, put the bung back in, found the oars where he had hidden them, and rowed back to his island.

A few days after his return, when he was preparing to go fishing, he paused briefly in his walk across the beach to look up to the rocky ridge behind his hut, now bathed in the evening light. There for a matter of seconds, he saw the short, dark stranger, sharply drawn against the crags. The sight both frightened and angered him, for his nature was to respond to fear with anger. He dropped the tub containing his fishing lines which he was carrying and lunged towards the figure. And as he moved the stranger was gone, leaving only the rocks of the ridge in the waning light.

"Ah," he said aloud, as was his custom. "That's it, then. You are just loneliness—just something a man or a boy will see who is too much by himself. Well, that is the end of you. You will not be on this island anymore. For I have now the boy, and he has me. We are God's gifts to each other, for He does not forget even sparrows like us."

He picked up his tub of lines and went down to the boat, thinking of the boy.

"He will make a great fisherman," he said. "He is small but he has courage. That is what matters. Everything is in the heart."

And with that he launched the boat and put out into the darkening sea to fish.

## THE END